LEGO® MAN in space

A TRUE STORY

written and illustrated by

MARA SHAUGHNESSY

Sky Pony Press
New York

WARNING

NO UNAUTHORIZED ENTRY BEYOND THIS POINT

For Mum
Thanks to Mat & Asad for being an inspiration to me and many others.
All my love to Jenn & Francis.

Sky Pony Press books may be purchased in bulk at special discounts for sales promotion, corporate gifts, fund-raising, or educational purposes. Special editions can also be created to specifications. For details, contact the Special Sales Department, Sky Pony Press, 307 West 36th Street, 11th Floor, New York, NY 10018 or info@skyhorsepublishing.com.

Sky Pony® is a registered trademark of Skyhorse Publishing, Inc.®, a Delaware corporation.

LEGO® is a trademark of the LEGO Group of companies which does not sponsor, authorize, or endorese this book.

Visit our website at www.skyponypress.com.

10 9 8 7 6 5 4 3 2

Printed in China

Library of Congress Cataloging-in-Publication Data is available on file.

ISBN: 978-1-62087-544-5

LEGO® MAN in space

A TRUE STORY

How did YOU get in here? You're not allowed to be here! Launching LEGO Man in Space is the work of highly trained and very important adults. No children allowed!

NATIONAL LEGONAUTICS & SPACE EXPLORATION FACILITIES

Nadia Skripochka
Astrophysicist
Kelvin Winklebottom
Aerospace Engineer
Farouk Fildzan
Director, Mission Control
Cola

Why are you still here? GO AWAY! Can't you see we're all very busy with the launch of LEGO Man in Space?
Um, excuse me?

Down here!

Grown-ups didn't send LEGO Man into space! That's not how it happened at all! I should know . . .

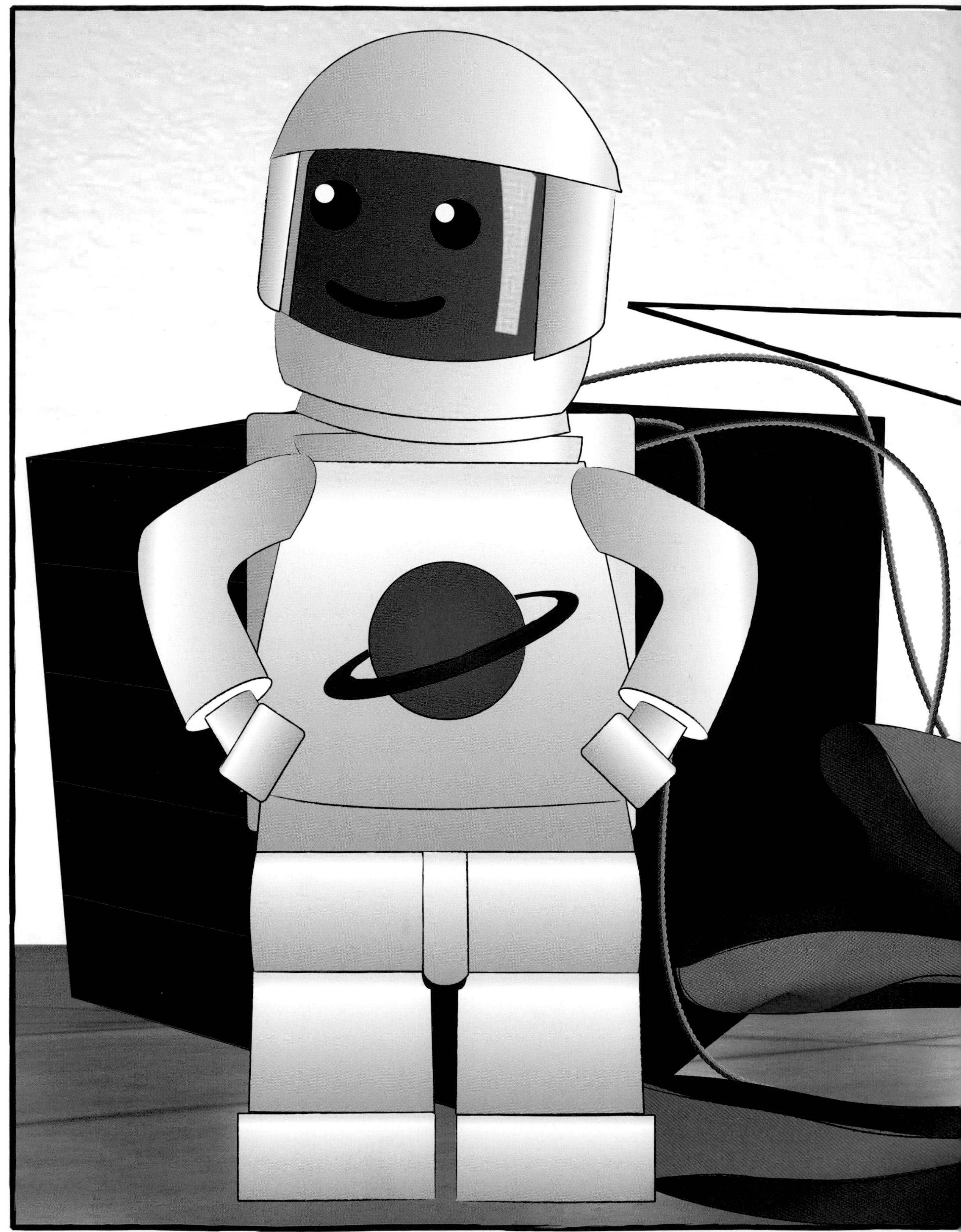

I'm

LEGO MAN IN SPACE

Can you guess how I got into space?

In a rocket ship?

A giant slingshot?

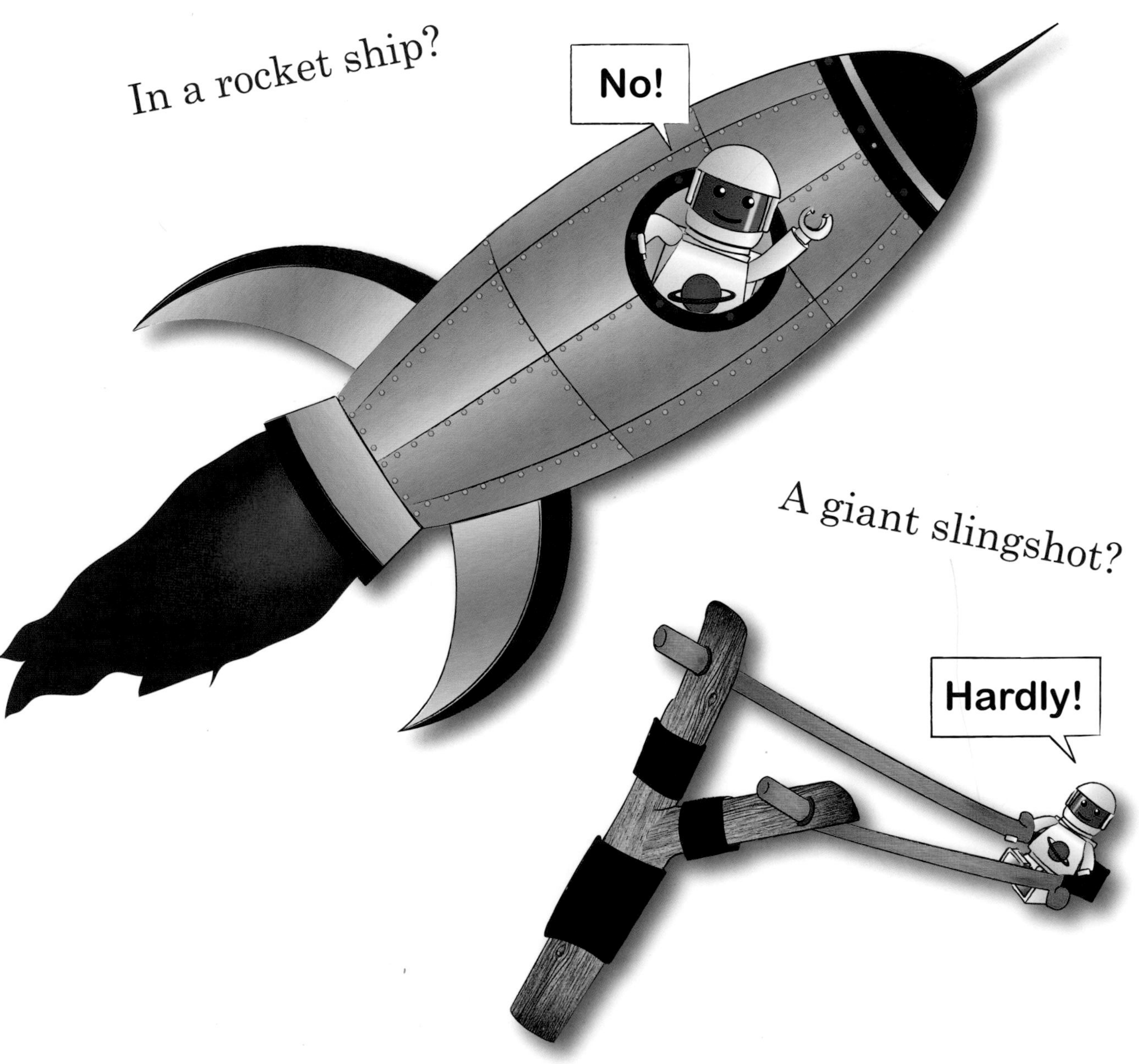

A catapult?

Caught a ride with a Martian?

Shot out of a cannon?

A pogo-stick?

It all started here. In this school hallway. With two kids who are just like you. Mat and Asad and their brilliant idea!

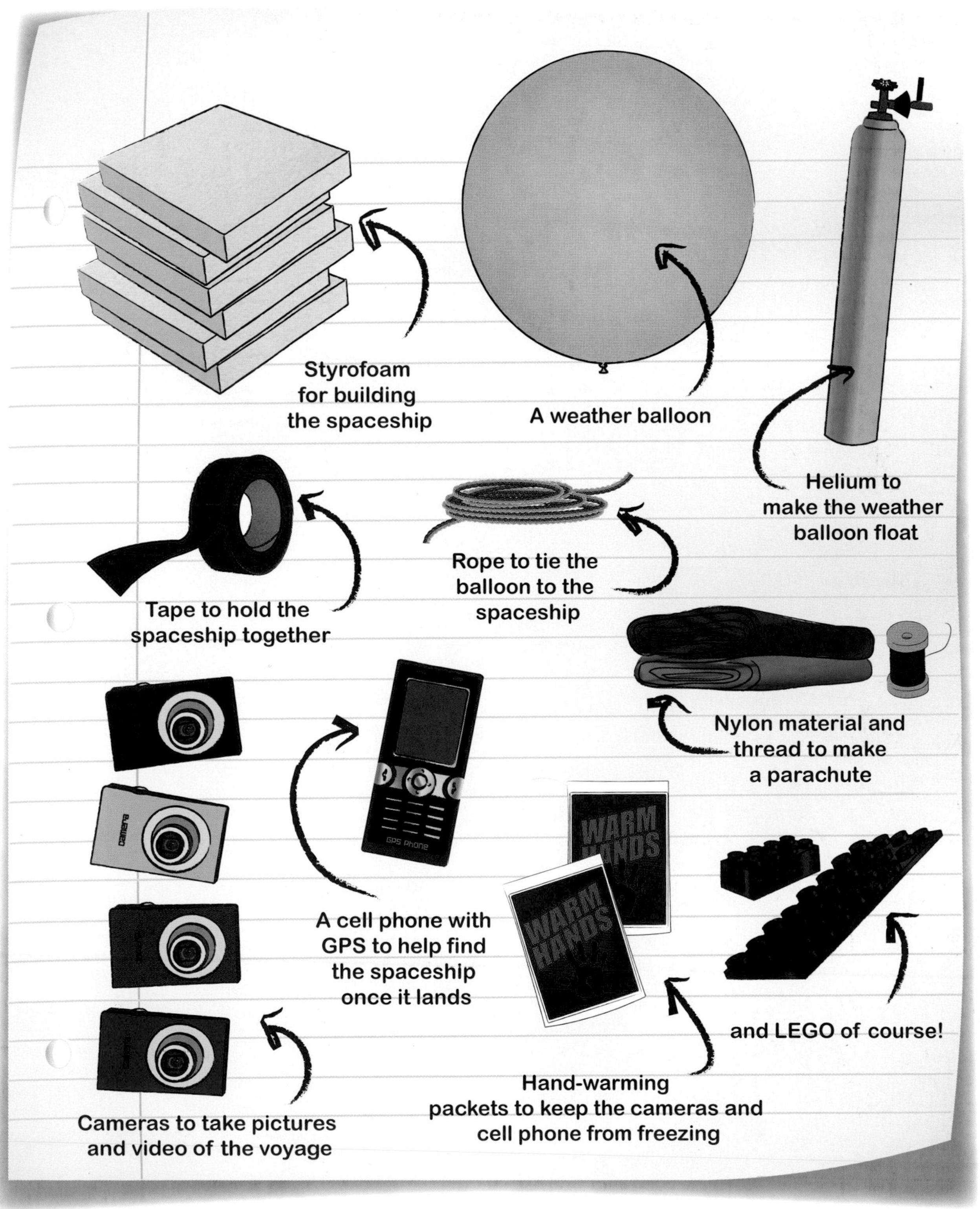

Mat and Asad made a list of the things they would need to send me into space.

With their materials, they built a
spaceship that looked like this.

They sewed a parachute to bring
me back to Earth safely.

Mat and Asad filled the ship's giant balloon with helium. They waited for just the right moment for my space launch. 3! 2! 1! Liftoff!

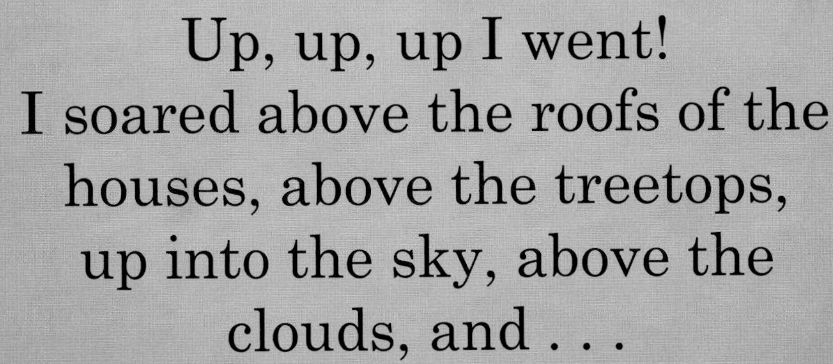

Up, up, up I went!
I soared above the roofs of the
houses, above the treetops,
up into the sky, above the
clouds, and . . .

Up into space! I saw the stars and the Moon and felt the Sun's very bright rays on my face. But the higher I went, the colder it got.

It got so cold that my balloon burst!
I went tumbling down, down, down.

Luckily, my spaceship's parachute opened.
And I floated safely back to Earth.

When Mat and Asad came to find me, they felt very proud of what they had done. I am proud too! Two kids plus one big idea . . . made me the LEGO Man in Space!

Did you know that the balloon that took me into space was as wide as a school bus and had enough helium inside to fill 600 party balloons? Do you want to see how high the balloon took me?

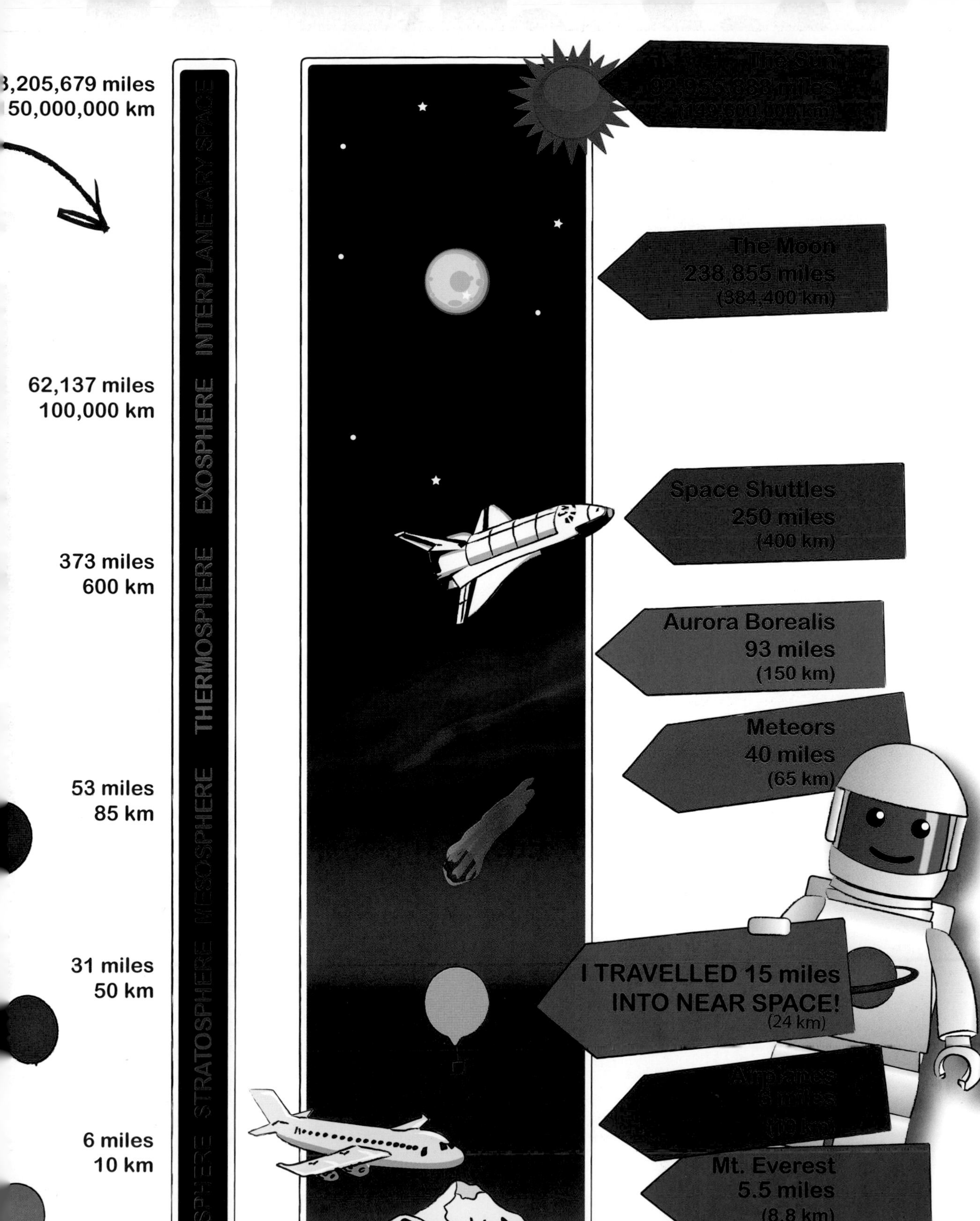

,205,679 miles
50,000,000 km
62,137 miles
100,000 km
373 miles
600 km
53 miles
85 km
31 miles
50 km
6 miles
10 km
TROPOSPHERE
STRATOSPHERE
MESOSPHERE
THERMOSPHERE
EXOSPHERE
INTERPLANETARY SPACE
The Sun
(149,600,000 km)
The Moon
238,855 miles
(384,400 km)
Space Shuttles
250 miles
(400 km)
Aurora Borealis
93 miles
(150 km)
Meteors
40 miles
(65 km)
I TRAVELLED 15 miles
INTO NEAR SPACE!
(24 km)
Airplanes
6 miles
(10 km)
Mt. Everest
5.5 miles
(8.8 km)
Birds
492 feet
(150 m)

Do you want to build a balloon-powered rocket ship for your own LEGO Man in Space?

Here's what you'll need:

- A milk carton
- A straw
- String
- Balloons
- Tape
- Scissors
- Glue
- Markers
- Aluminum foil, tissue paper, buttons, and odds and ends for decorating

1. Cut the bottom from your milk carton and cut a window into the top. Ask an adult for help so you don't poke yourself with the scissors. Now decorate your spaceship.

2. Cut a 1-inch piece of straw. Tape it on the top of your rocket. Thread your string through the straw. Tie one end of your string to a chair. Tie the other end of your string to another chair.

3. Blow up your balloon inside the milk carton until it fills up all of the space.

4. 3! 2! 1! Blastoff! Release your balloon and watch your rocket ship zoom! Have a race with your friends to see how fast each of your rocket ships can go!

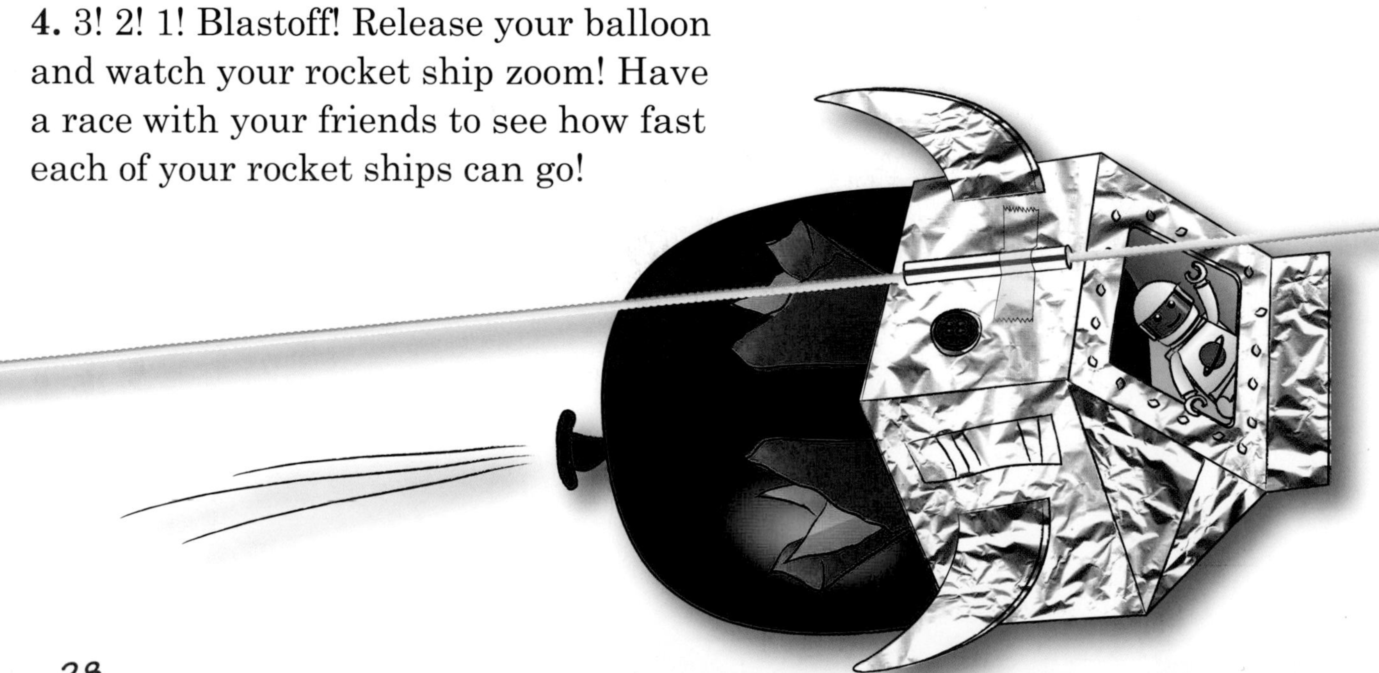

Do you want to make a parachute for your own LEGO Man in Space?

Here's what you'll need:

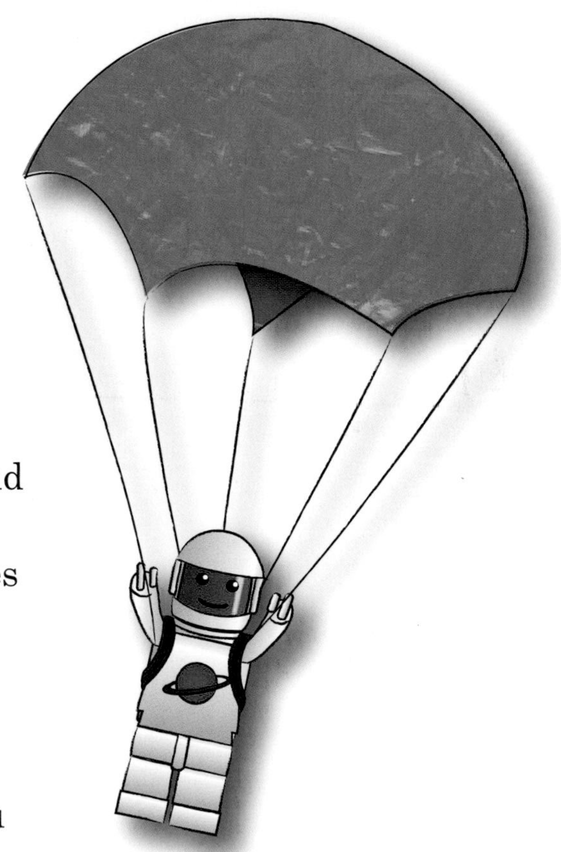

- String or thread
- Plastic shopping bag
- Tape

1. Cut a piece of plastic from your shopping bag. Circles, squares, and rectangles work well, but you can experiment with all sorts of shapes and sizes.

2. Carefully poke holes into the edges or corners. Thread lengths of string into each of the holes you have made and tie with a knot. Attach each length of the string to your LEGO man.

3. Go ahead and test out your parachute! Remember to ask an adult for permission to try out your parachute from anywhere up high.

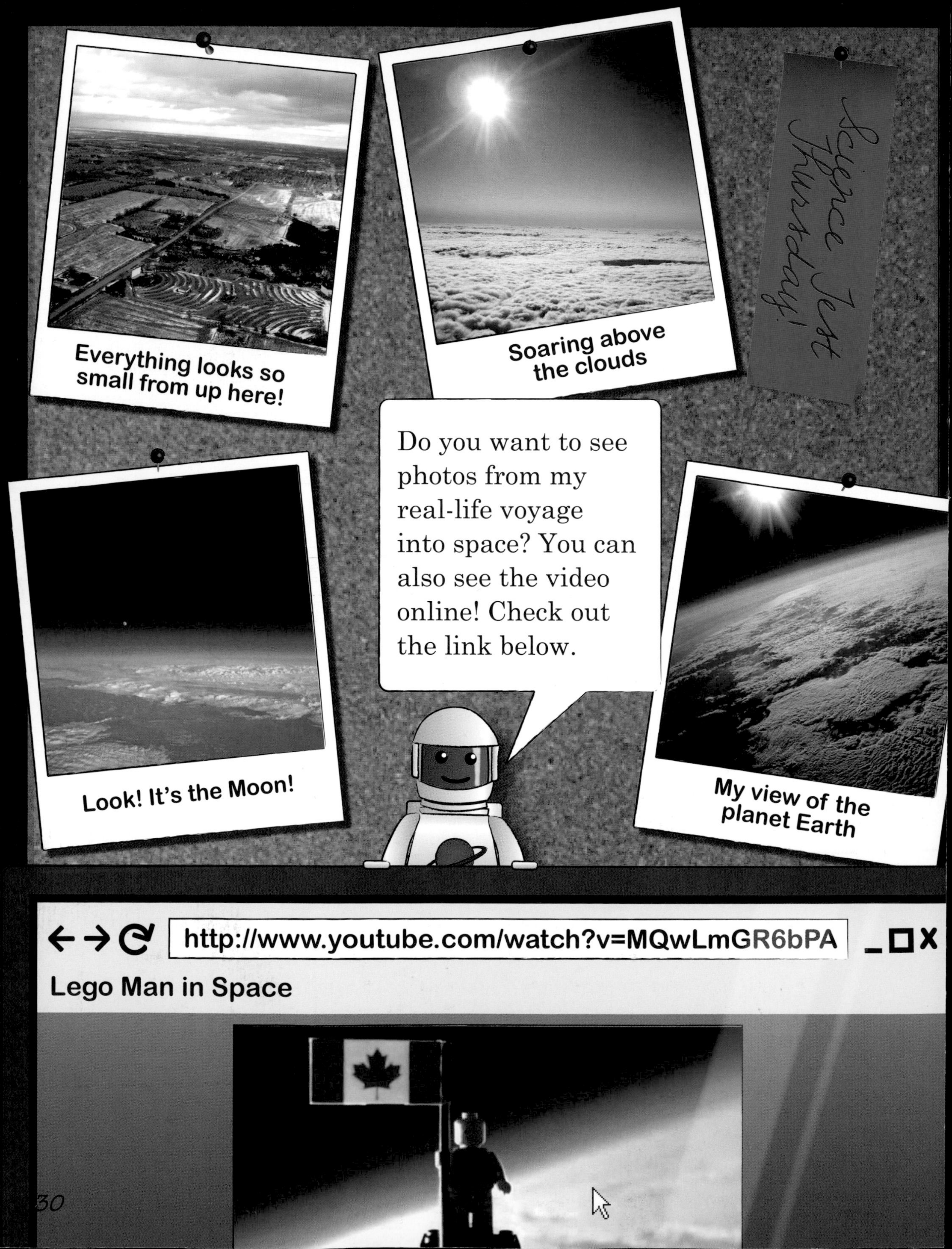

Everything looks so small from up here!

Soaring above the clouds

Science Test Thursday!

Do you want to see photos from my real-life voyage into space? You can also see the video online! Check out the link below.

Look! It's the Moon!

My view of the planet Earth

More Fun Activities!

Do you want to draw your own LEGO man? All you need are three simple shapes! Now add some color!

Onomatomania—A great-sounding creative writing assignment. Onomatopoeia is a big long word that means "a word that SOUNDS like a sound." You have seen four examples of onomatopoeia in this book: *Boing! Boing! Boing!*; *Ka-boom!*; *Pop!*; and *Pssssst!* Write a list of ten words that imitate a sound (try *zoom* or *buzz* to get your list started). Next, write a story about traveling into space. How many of the words from your list can you fit into your story?

Mission Blastoff—A far out phys ed game. Spread out several hula hoops in the middle of the play space. There should be fewer hula hoops than players. Each astronaut starts off in a crouched position around the perimeter of the play space. The leader of the game shouts "3! 2! 1! Blastoff!" Astronauts leap as high as they can into the air and begin orbiting the play space, walking as quickly as they can. The leader shouts out "Low gravity!" at which point astronauts must walk and jump in slow motion. The leader shouts out "Prepare for landing!" at which point the astronauts must rush to land on a planet (jump inside a hula hoop). Uh-oh! Only one astronaut per planet. Any astronauts who are unable to land must return to mission control (a designated place of your choosing) and complete 5 exercises to recharge their spaceships (5 wall push-ups, 5 sit-ups, 5 jumping jacks, etc.) and re-enter for the next round of Mission Blastoff.

Can I get a lift?—A weighty math problem. A balloon filled with helium has the ability to lift ½ ounce (14 grams) into the air. A LEGO man weighs 0.07 ounces (2 grams). How many of these LEGO men and women could be lifted by a single balloon? Look for other objects in the classroom or at home. How much do they weigh? How many balloons would you need to lift your objects off the ground?

Links and Online Resources

http://www.youtube.com/watch?v=MQwLmGR6bPA

Want to watch the LEGO Man shoot upwards into near space? Check out the stunning views as he soars out of the neighborhood, past the clouds, and drifts high above the Earth.

http://www.youtube.com/watch?v=Lum1DMTdccE

Watch the LEGO Man in Space news story created by *The National*, a news program from Canada's public television broadcaster, CBC.

http://teachingkidsnews.com/2012/01/29/toronto-teens-send-legonaut-into-near-space/

Teaching Kids News uses real news articles as a starting point for lessons in the classroom. Check out some interesting grammar, literacy, and investigative learning ideas for the classroom based on the *Toronto Star* article about LEGO Man in Space.

http://www.nasa.gov/audience/forkids/kidsclub/flash/index.html

The NASA *Kids' Club* website has all sorts of fun space things to explore: educational space-themed games and activities, interactive images of the Earth taken from space, a computerized scientist designed to answer your questions, information about astronauts, and lots of kid-sized NASA challenges.

http://pbskids.org/zoom/activities/sci/

PBS Kids hosts tons of fabulous science, physics, and engineering activities for kids. Check out the "Engineering: Design It" section for ideas on how to build a mechanical arm, a balloon-powered craft that blasts off, and a hovercraft that really works. Check out the "Forces & Energy: Move It" section for a rocket fueled by lemon juice and baking soda, a hot air balloon craft, and a mini-sized glider.

http://kids.yahoo.com/science

Yahoo! Kids hosts great information about the solar system and space stations. Kids can explore the glossary section for detailed and full explanations of all-things-space terminology. Don't forget to check out the space exploration videos while you're there too!

http://www.spacefoundation.org/education

Space Foundation has all sorts of space-themed craft and snack ideas. Create your own alien out of things you find around the house, design and build a rover for planetary exploration, or make an "out of this world" Martian snack.

http://search.nasa.gov/search/edFilterSearch.jsp?empty=true

NASA Education provides an incredible bank of resources for teachers to use in their classrooms. Tailor your search by grade and subtopic and be amazed to discover literally hundreds of lessons, from "Astronaut Food" to "How to Space Walk" to "Careers in Space Exploration."

http://kids.discovery.com/tell-me/space and http://www.discoveryeducation.com

Discovery Kids hosts a great site with kid-friendly explanations for things like "How do rocket engines work?" and "Why are space suits so important?" Its sister site, Discovery Education has great space science lessons like how Earth and Mars are alike but different and how to build a planetarium in your classroom. You can also find printable, space-themed worksheets.